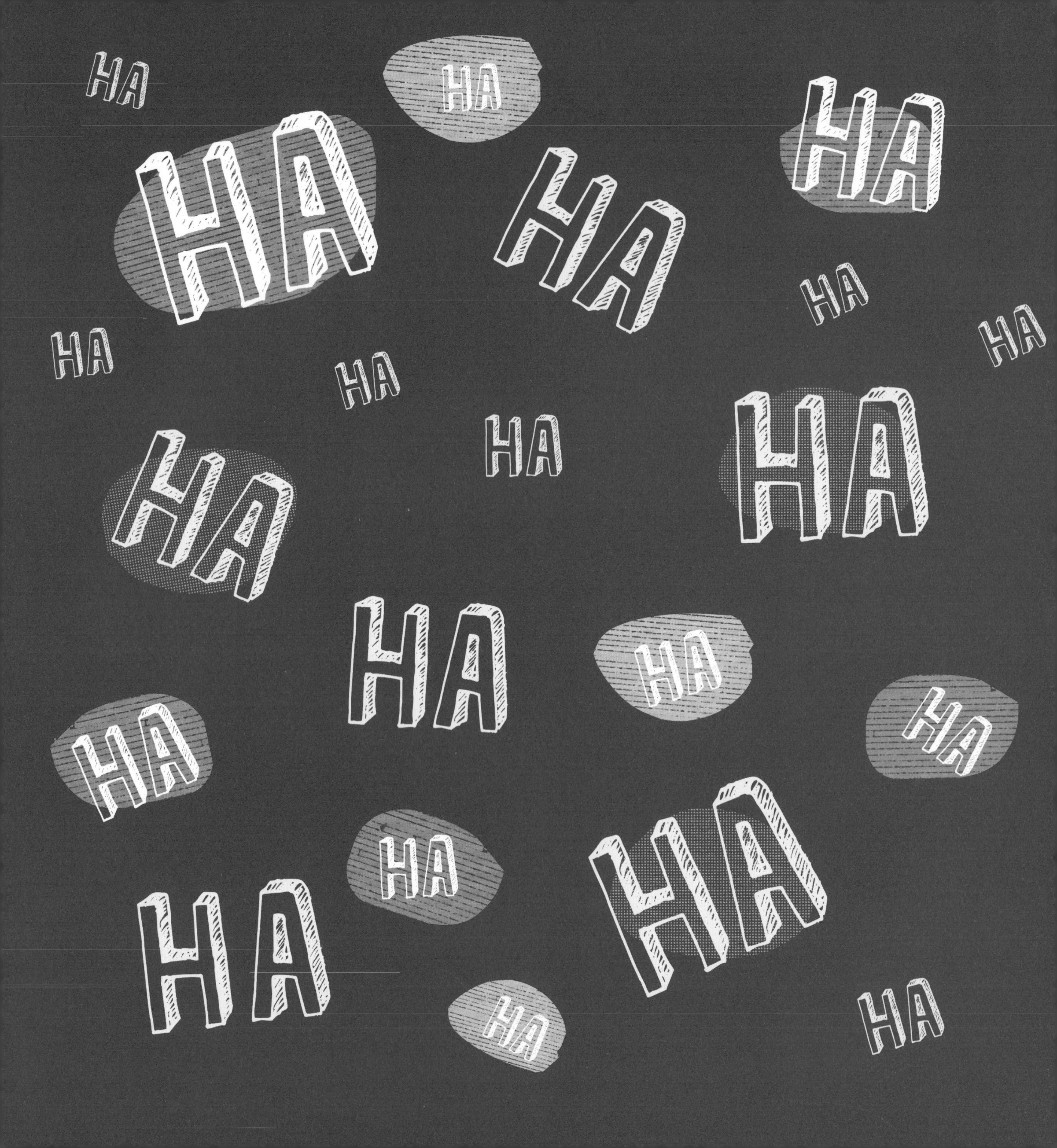
HA
HA
HA
HA
HA
HA
HA
HA
HA
HA
HA
HA
HA
HA
HA
HA
HA
HA
HA
HA
HA

STOP! STOP!! STOP!!!

If you are about to read this book to someone, then please follow these

VERY IMPORTANT RULES

1. <u>DON'T</u> LOOK AT THIS BOOK! (I mean—except to know what words to say.) Also, don't look at your beautiful fingernails.

Instead...

2. <u>DO</u> LOOK AT YOUR LISTENER! Gaze DEEEEEP into their eyes. Give them LOOOOONG, SUPER-serious stares. Go NUTS when they say something silly!

And also...

3. GET YOUR LISTENER TO LOOK AT <u>YOU</u>! Yes, they'll want to admire your beautiful fingernails, but DON'T LET THEM!

And remember, if they laugh...

You're starting this book over!

OKAY, KID . . .

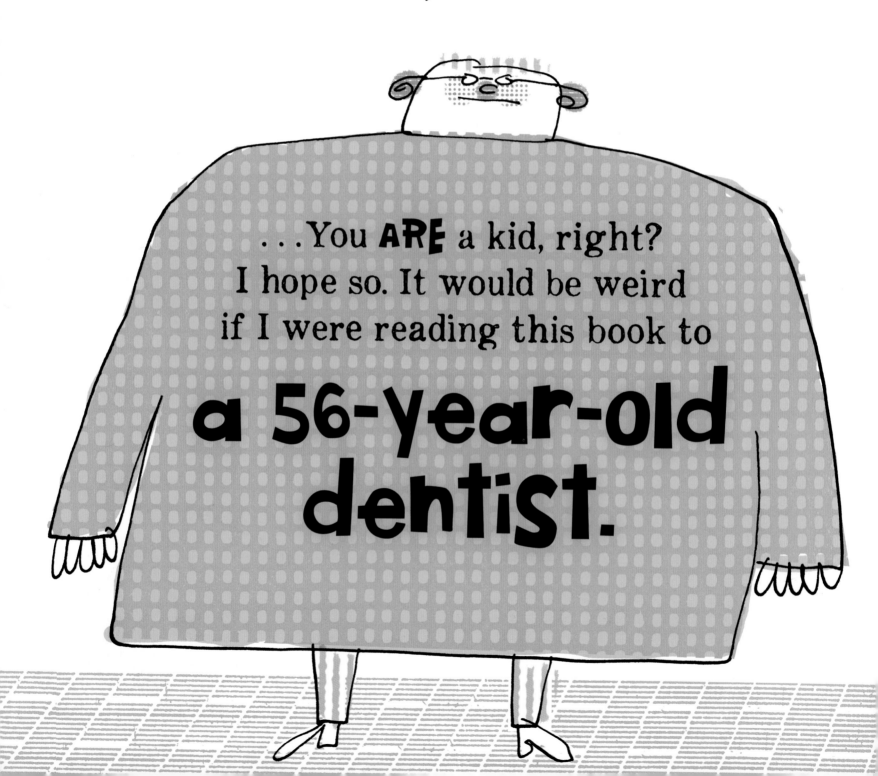

. . .You **ARE** a kid, right?
I hope so. It would be weird
if I were reading this book to

a 56-year-old dentist.

You're not a **56-year-old dentist**, are you?
Or maybe you're a large pineapple
dressed in children's clothes?
You really are a kid?
Okay. If you **promise**
you're a kid,
then let's turn the page.

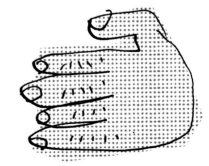

Here's the deal. I have something
that I really want to tell you. It's a

BIG THING.

And it's **very serious.**
That's why I'm giving you this VERY SERIOUS look right now.

LOOK AT MY FACE.

Doesn't it look serious?

Before I tell you that **big thing**, I have to make sure that
you're in a serious mood, too. So please, **no laughing**
while I read you this book. BeCauSe . . .

If You LAUGH,

The illustrations for this book were
created using ink on paper with digital color and photo enhancements and
a lot of fun. This book was edited by Andrea Spooner and designed by Véronique Lefèvre Sweet
and Christine Kettner. The production was supervised by Kimberly Stella, and the production editor was Annie
McDonnell. The text was set in Appareo Medium, and the display types are LD Funky Chunky and Pusekatt regular.

· Little, Brown and Company · Hachette Book Group · 1290 Avenue of the Americas · New York, NY 10104 · Visit us at LBYR.com · First Edition: September 2022 · Little, Brown and Company is a division of Hachette Book Group, Inc. The Little, Brown name and logo are trademarks of Hachette Book Group, Inc. · The publisher is not responsible for websites (or their content) that are not owned by the publisher. · Library of Congress Cataloging-in-Publication Data · Names: Harris, Chris, 1970– author. | Bloch, Serge, illustrator. · Title: If you laugh, I'm starting this book over / written by Chris Harris ; illustrated by Serge Bloch. · Other titles: If you laugh, I am starting this book over · Description: First edition. | New York : Little, Brown and Company, 2022. | Audience: Ages 4–8. | Summary: "Readers are challenged not to laugh in a series of increasingly hilarious prompts and jokes that lead to a serious message about the pleasures of laughter"— Provided by publisher. · Identifiers: LCCN 2021048977 | ISBN 9780316424882 (hardcover) · Subjects: CYAC: Laughter—Fiction. | Humorous stories. | LCGFT: Picture books. · Classification: LCC PZ7.1.H37463 If 2022 | DDC [Fic]—dc23 · LC record available at https://lccn.loc.gov/2021048977 · ISBN 978-0-316-42488-2 · PRINTED IN CHINA · APS · 10 9 8 7 6 5 4 3 2 1

I'm Starting This Book OVER

Written by **Chris Harris**
Illustrated by **Serge Bloch**

Now we'll start.
And remember,
from here on
out, DO NOT LAUGH.
If I hear you laugh,
then I'll go right
back to page one
and say...

L B
Little, Brown and Company
New York Boston

NO NO NO, YOU GIGGLY GOOSE, WHY DID YOU LAUGH?

Now we have to Start the book over!!!

And look where we are now: good ol' **PAGE ONE**.

Please—please—PLEASE, let's try to never see this page again, all right?

1

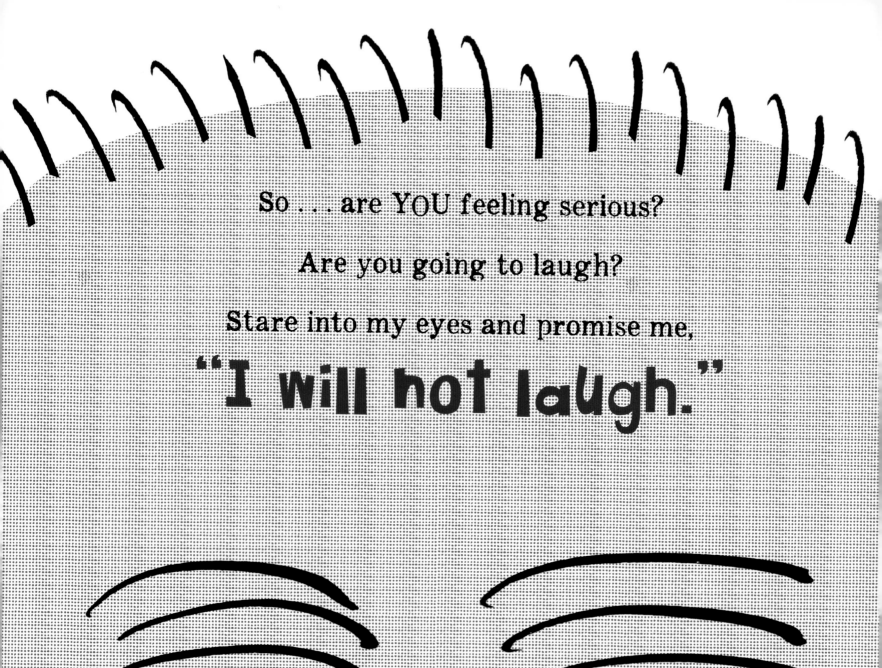

So . . . are YOU feeling serious?

Are you going to laugh?

Stare into my eyes and promise me,

"I will not laugh."

Whoa, that was too fast. Stare right
into my giant eyeballs and say it more slowly:

"IIIIIIII wiiiiiiIIIIII
hooooooooot
laaaaaaaaaaaaaaaaaaaaugh."

(Go ahead!
Say it!)

GOOD JOB!

But...everyone knows that
to make a **REALLY** serious
promise, you cover your mouth
and say it in a super-squeaky
mouse voice, like this:

I. Will. Not. Laugh.

So please do that now.

What a great Start! I'm So glad you haven't laughed yet.

Because this is so serious, I think we need to use our **real nameS** to promise each other we won't laugh. Have I ever told you my real name? This is a pretty **big SecreT**, so please take it seriously. My real name is actually...

Chicken McStinkbreath Eyeball.

Do you know what **YOUR** real name is?
Your real name is actually . . .

Captain Funnyhair Snozzdripple.

Now repeat after me:
"We, McStinkbreath and Funnyhair . . .

promise
NOT
to laugh."

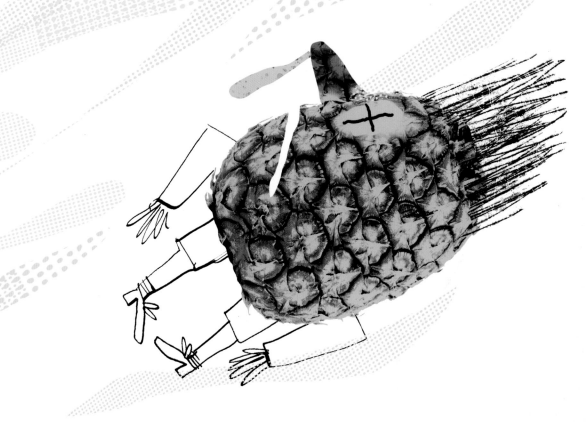

That's good, but I need to stare deeply into your eyes to see if you really mean what you promised. Keep verrrry still.

Here we go!

I'M LOOKING . . .

I'M LOOKING . . .

WHOA.
You have a lot of WEIRD thoughts.

Wait...are you thinking that...I'm a **Silly person?**
And you think I'm silly because...I'm scared of
Cute Yellow feathers?

They're scary!

Um, hello, don't you know that **everyone**
is scared of cute yellow feathers?

Hold on. Now you're thinking . . .
that my head looks like a
giant cheeseburger?

Why Are You Thinking That?!

And you're also thinking that I probably use ketchup as my **Shampoo?** That's ridiculous— I've only done that three times in my **whole life.**

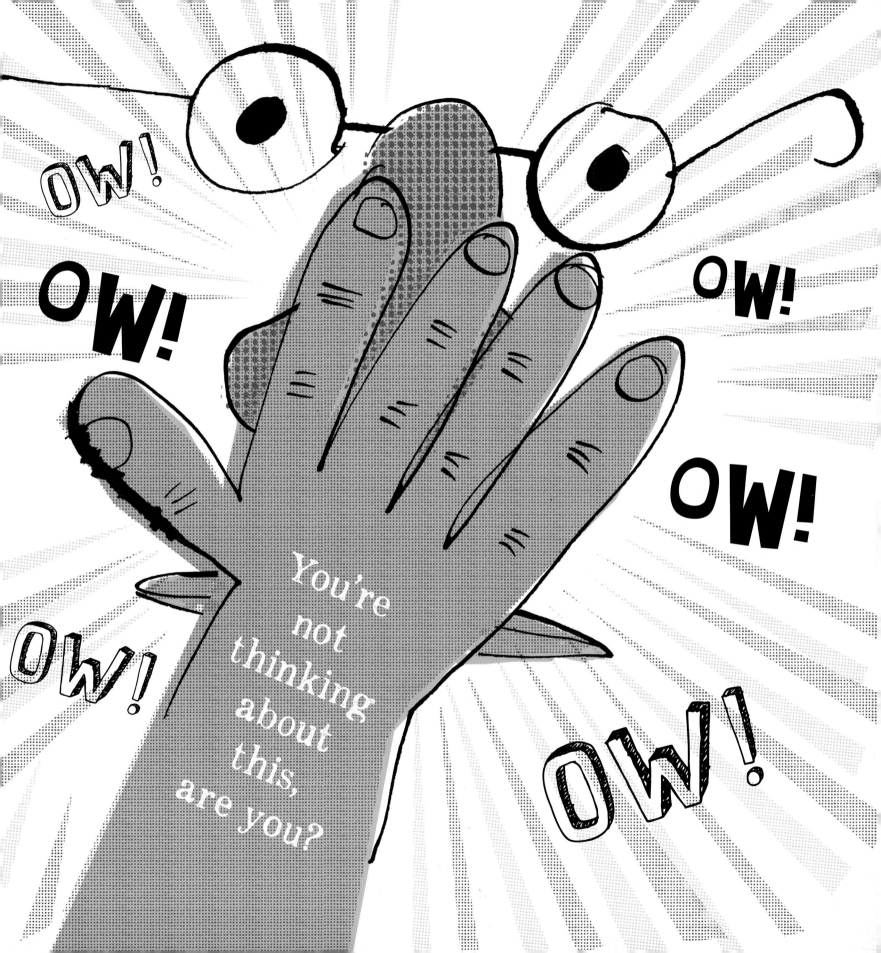

UH-OH.

I can tell that you're about to laugh. Quick, think about something serious. Maybe something scary, like . . . **a cute yellow feather!**

Tickle Tickle

Wait, I have a better idea. Staplers aren't funny, are they?

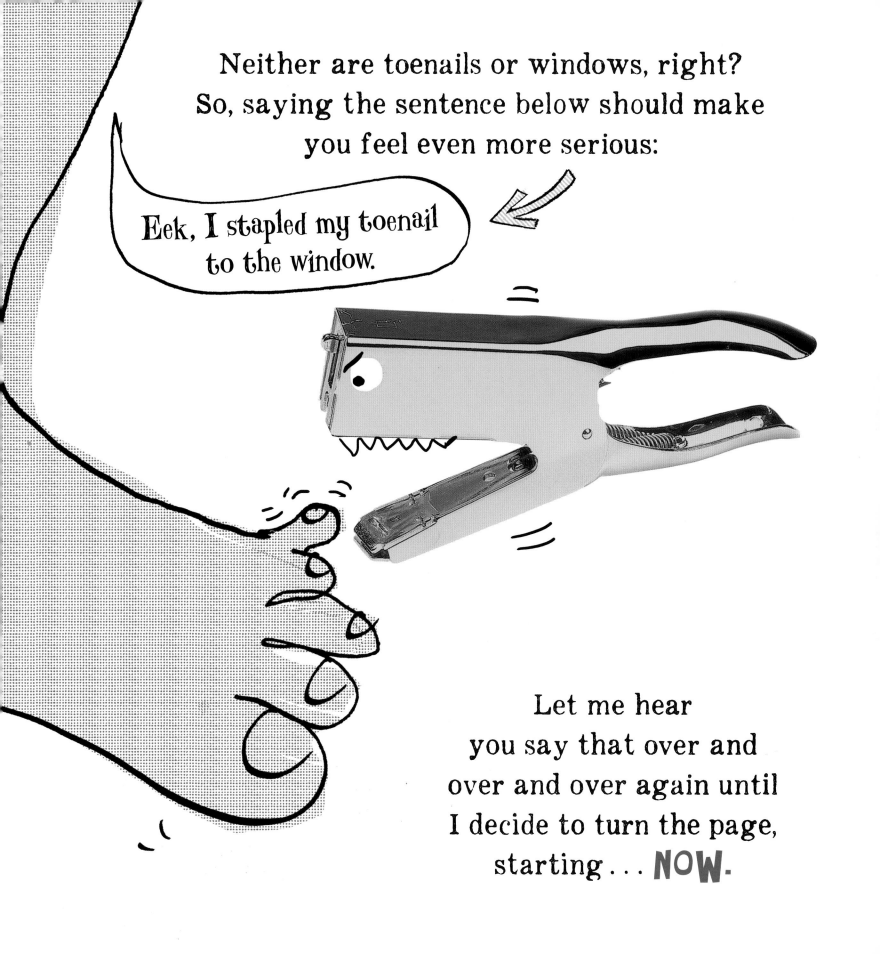

WOW, YOU'RE INCREDIBLE!

I have one last request before I tell you the **BIG THING.** To prove that you're really feeling serious, all you have to do— and this is really easy—is just float up in the air about three feet off the ground.

You can start floating... NOW!

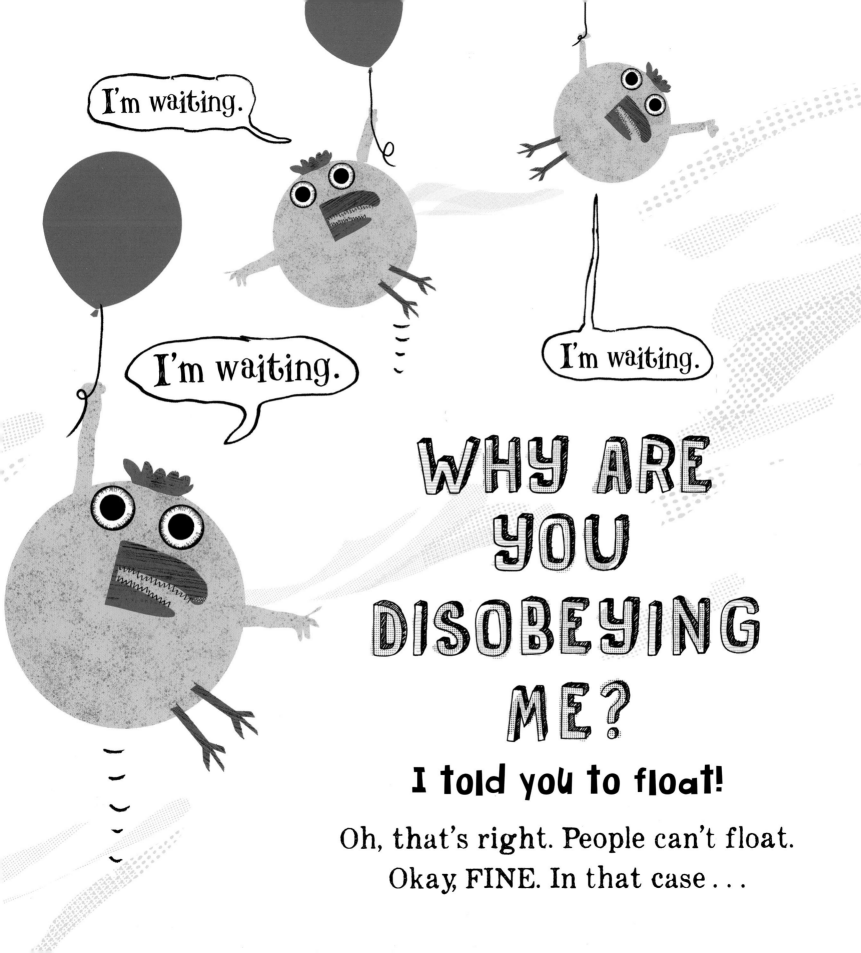

So here's the

BIG THING

that I want to tell you.

Do you know what
the best sound in the world is?
The best sound in the world is,
by far . . .

. . . the sound of your laughter.

WHAT?! I know.

Then why the heck have I been telling you **NOT** to laugh? Because I want to make sure you understand how much I mean it. Your laughter is the most wonderful sound there is. It's more beautiful than—hmm, what's the most beautiful thing I can think of? It's more beautiful than . . .

. . . a really, really **Smelly pair** of sneakers.

It's more
joyful than . . .

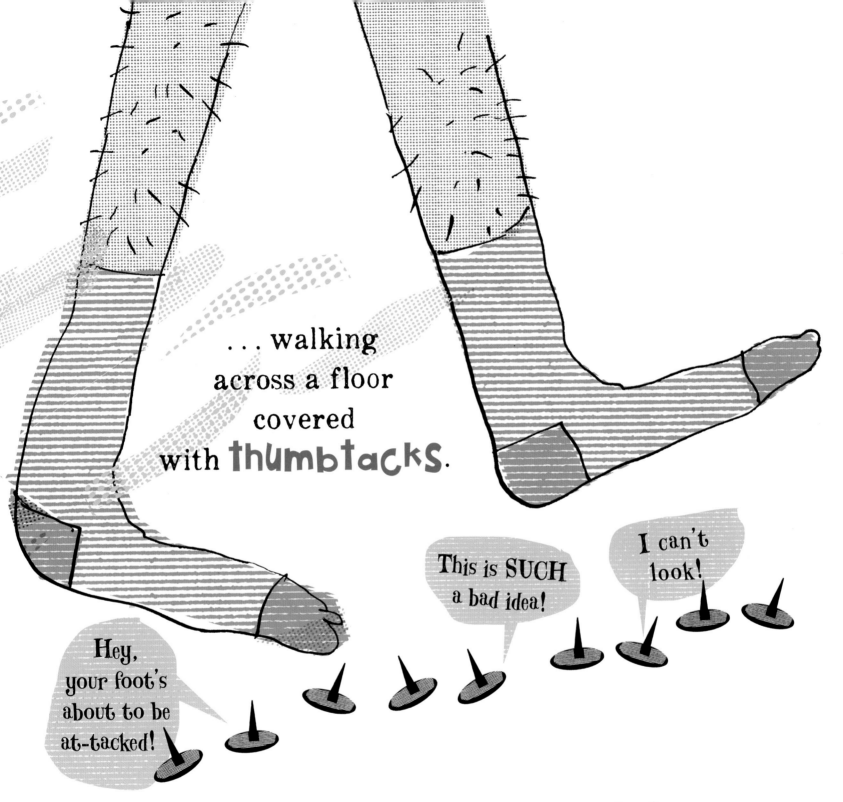

... walking across a floor covered with **thumbtacks**.

And I would never trade a second of your laughter for **anything**. Not even for . . .

...the oldest pile of mashed potatoes in the world.

Your laughter makes the world a happier place for everyone around you. And I mean that **seriously.**

OH NO look out it's EVERYONE RUN

Huh. I guess maybe yellow feathers aren't THAT scary.

a scary yellow feather

FOR YOUR LIVES!!!!

Why didn't you tell me that? Anyway, where was I? Oh, right . . .

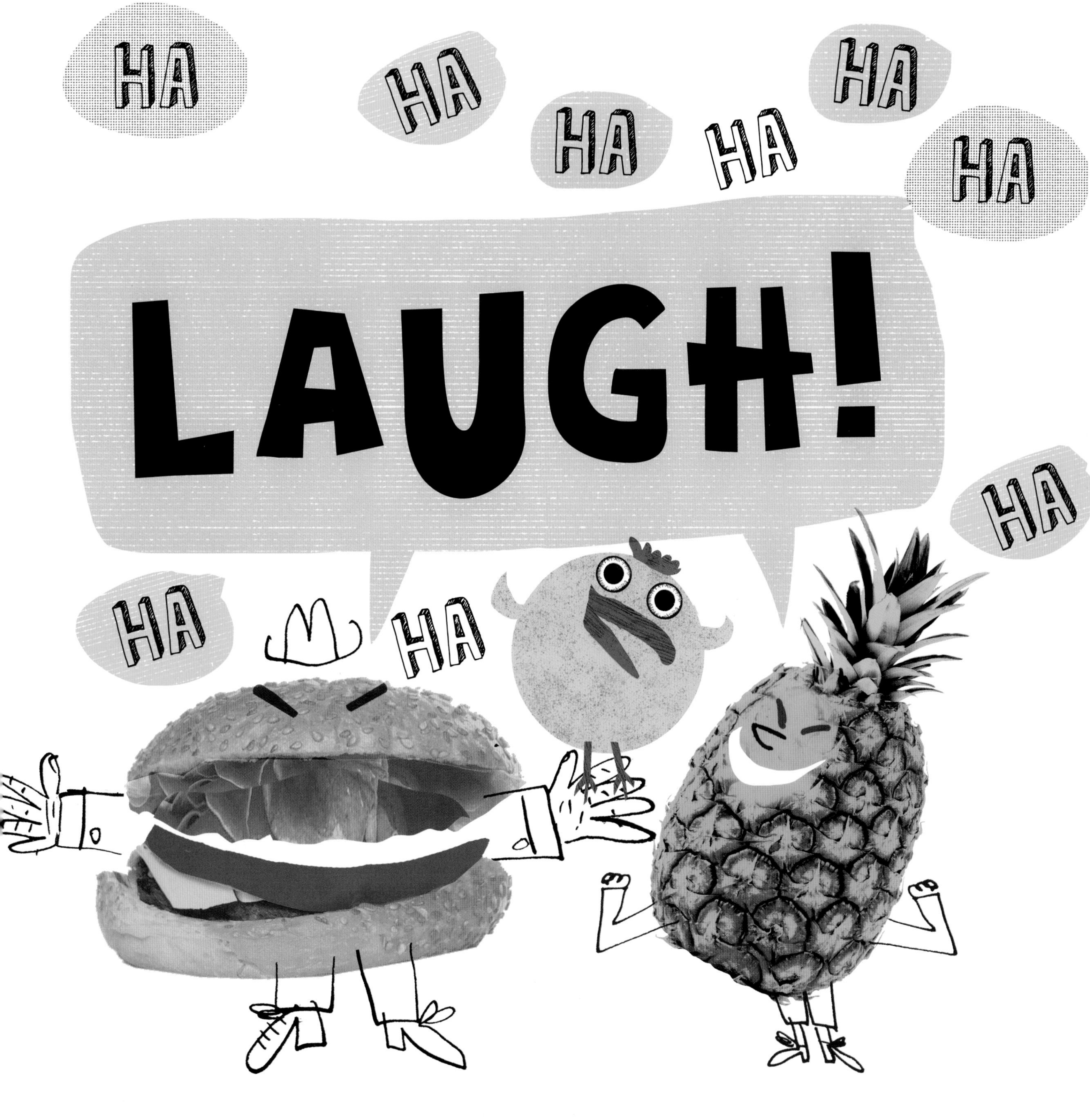
HA
HA
HA
HA
HA
HA
LAUGH!
HA
HA
HA

P.S.: From here on out, you're not allowed to **STOP laughing.** In fact, if you ever stop laughing, then you have to give me **one million dollars.** I'm sorry, but that's the rule. So . . .

KEEP LAUGHING! . . .
KEEP LAUGHING! . . .
KEEP LAUGHING! . . .
KEEP LAUGHING! . . .
KEEP LAUGHING! . . .

HA HA
HA HA
HA HA
HA HA HA HA
HA HA HA
HA HA

HA HA
HA
HA HA
HA
HA HA
HA
HA HA
HA
HA HA
HA
HA HA
HA